Dear Parents:

Congratulations! Your child is taking
the first steps on an exciting journey.
The destination? Independent reading!

STEP INTO READING® will help your child get there. The program offers
five steps to reading success. Each step includes fun stories and colorful
art or photographs. In addition to original fiction and books with favorite
characters, there are Step into Reading Non-Fiction Readers, Phonics Readers
and Boxed Sets, Sticker Readers, and Comic Readers—a complete literacy
program with something to interest every child.

Learning to Read, Step by Step!

Ready to Read   Preschool–Kindergarten
• big type and easy words • rhyme and rhythm • picture clues
For children who know the alphabet and are eager to
begin reading.

Reading with Help   Preschool–Grade 1
• basic vocabulary • short sentences • simple stories
For children who recognize familiar words and sound out
new words with help.

Reading on Your Own   Grades 1–3
• engaging characters • easy-to-follow plots • popular topics
For children who are ready to read on their own.

Reading Paragraphs   Grades 2–3
• challenging vocabulary • short paragraphs • exciting stories
For newly independent readers who read simple sentences
with confidence.

Ready for Chapters   Grades 2–4
• chapters • longer paragraphs • full-color art
For children who want to take the plunge into chapter books
but still like colorful pictures.

STEP INTO READING® is designed to give every child a successful
reading experience. The grade levels are only guides; children will progress
through the steps at their own speed, developing confidence in their reading.

Remember, a lifetime love of reading starts with a single step!

To Isaiah, who is always ready to race
—B.W.

  Copyright © 2023 DC & WBEI. BATWHEELS and all related characters and elements © & ™ DC and Warner Bros. Entertainment Inc. WB SHIELD: © & ™ WBEI. (s23)

Visit us on the Web!
StepIntoReading.com
rhcbooks.com

Educators and librarians, for a variety of teaching tools, visit us at RHTeachersLibrarians.com

ISBN 978-0-593-57053-1 (trade) — ISBN 978-0-593-57054-8 (lib. bdg.)
ISBN 978-0-593-57055-5 (ebook)

Printed in the United States of America

10 9 8 7 6 5 4 3 2 1

STEP INTO READING®

STEP 1 READY TO READ

BAM AND THE BATWHEELS!

by Billy Wrecks

Batman created by Bob Kane with Bill Finger

Random House 🏠 New York

Shhhh . . . there is
a new secret group
of crime fighters
on the streets
of Gotham City.

They are the
Super Hero vehicles
known as . . .

. . . the Batwheels!

Bam is the Batmobile.
He is a rocket-powered
machine who can catch
Super-Villains and race
to the rescue when
people are in need.

Batman is a brave
Super Hero who
watches over
Gotham City
and protects it from
Super-Villains.

Bibi is a motorcycle. She weaves in and out of any tight spot with ease.

Batgirl is a whiz when it comes to computers and technology.

She loves to ride
her motorcycle.

Redbird is a red-hot sports car who loves to go fast.

Robin is

Batman's sidekick.

He likes
lots of speed
and action!

Batwing is a super-sonic jet who soars through the sky and keeps an eye on the Batwheels from above.

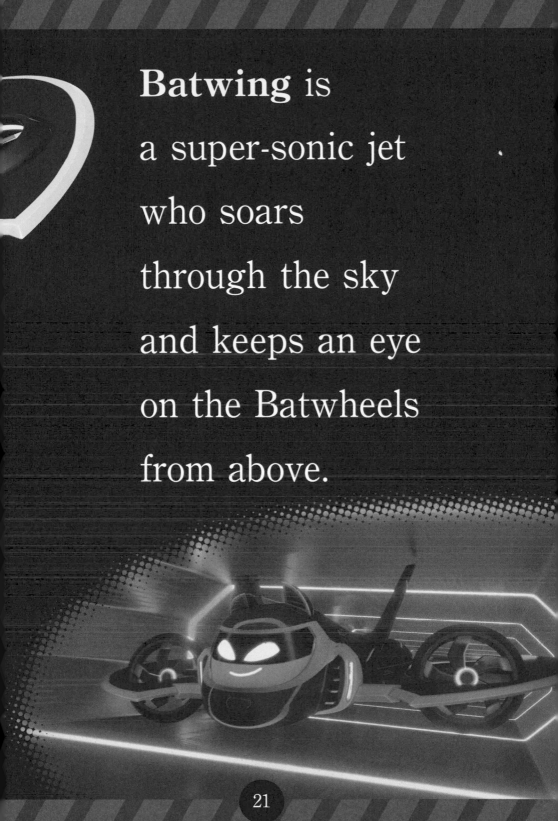

When things get tough,
the Batwheels call **Buff**.

This truck has
the big wheels
and brawn they
need to muscle
through any situation.

The Batwheels

rev their engines,
always ready
to save the day.
VROOM!